This Little Tiger book
belongs to:

_____

_____

_____

For Joey
– A. R.

To every child in this world who, because of war,
is deprived of a peaceful and playful childhood
– D. K.

LITTLE TIGER PRESS
An imprint of Magi Publications
1 The Coda Centre,
189 Munster Road, London SW6 6AW
www.littletigerpress.com

First published in Great Britain 2005
This edition published 2006

Text and illustrations
copyright © Magi Publications 2005

A CIP catalogue record for this book is available
from the British Library

All rights reserved • ISBN 1 84506 104 7

Printed in Singapore by Tien Wah Press Pte.

10 9 8 7 6 5 4 3 2 1

What Bear Likes Best!

Alison Ritchie

illustrated by

Dubravka Kolanovic

LITTLE TIGER PRESS
London

Bear was sunning himself
on his favourite hilltop.
He loved days like this —
nothing in particular to do
and nowhere in particular
to go.

Buzzzzzzzzz!

Buzzzz! A bee
landed on his nose.

"Get up, Bear," he said crossly.
"How can I collect pollen with bears
squashing my flowers?"
"Sorry, Bee," said Bear, laughing.

Bear curled himself up
and roly-polied down the hill.
Roly-polying was one of his
favourite things to do.

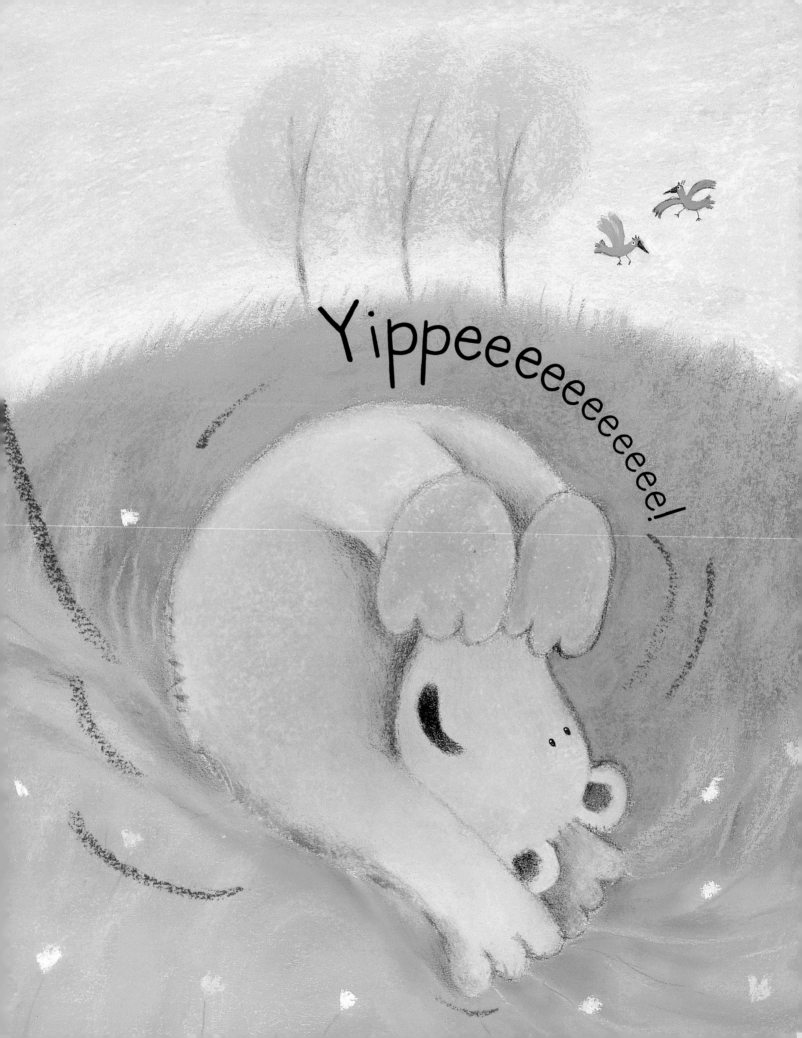

Oooof!

Bump! Bear landed on top
of something warm and furry.
"Oi!" gasped Mole. "How can I
dig holes with bears landing on me?"

"I'll help you!" said Bear. And he dug
and dug and dug.
"Stop! Stop! STOP!" cried Mole,
as mud flew everywhere.
"Sorry, Mole," said Bear and he
hurried away.

Bear ran towards the river
and splashed into the water.
Splashing was one of his
favourite things to do.

Splish
Splash

"Hey!" grumbled Heron. "How can I catch
fish with bears chasing them away?"
"Sorry, Heron," said Bear and he
bounced off to play somewhere else.

Blah!

Bear hopped across the stepping stones,
leapt on to the riverbank and ran into
the woods. It was time for a back scratch.
Scratching his back was one of his
favourite things to do.

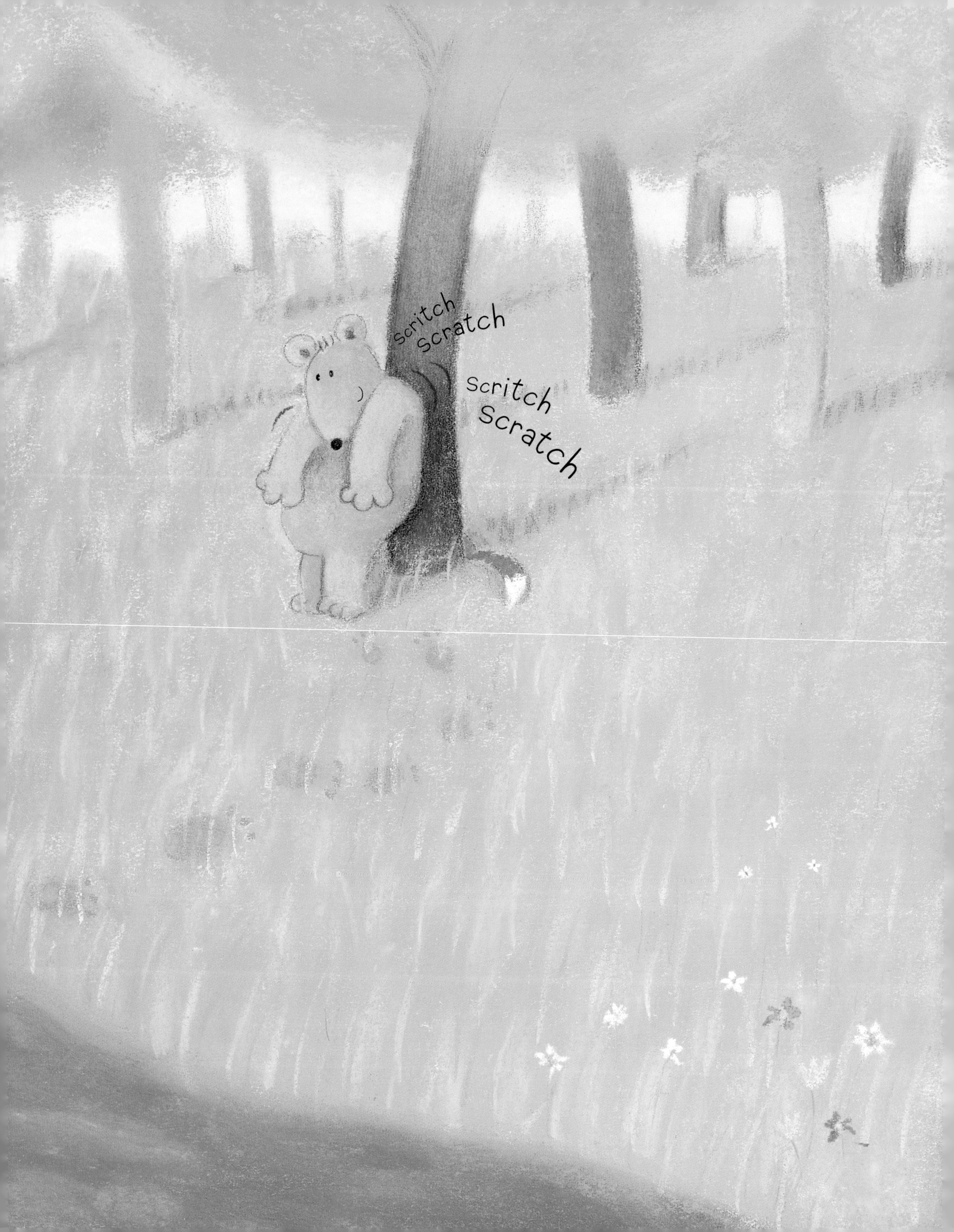
Scritch
Scratch
Scritch
Scratch

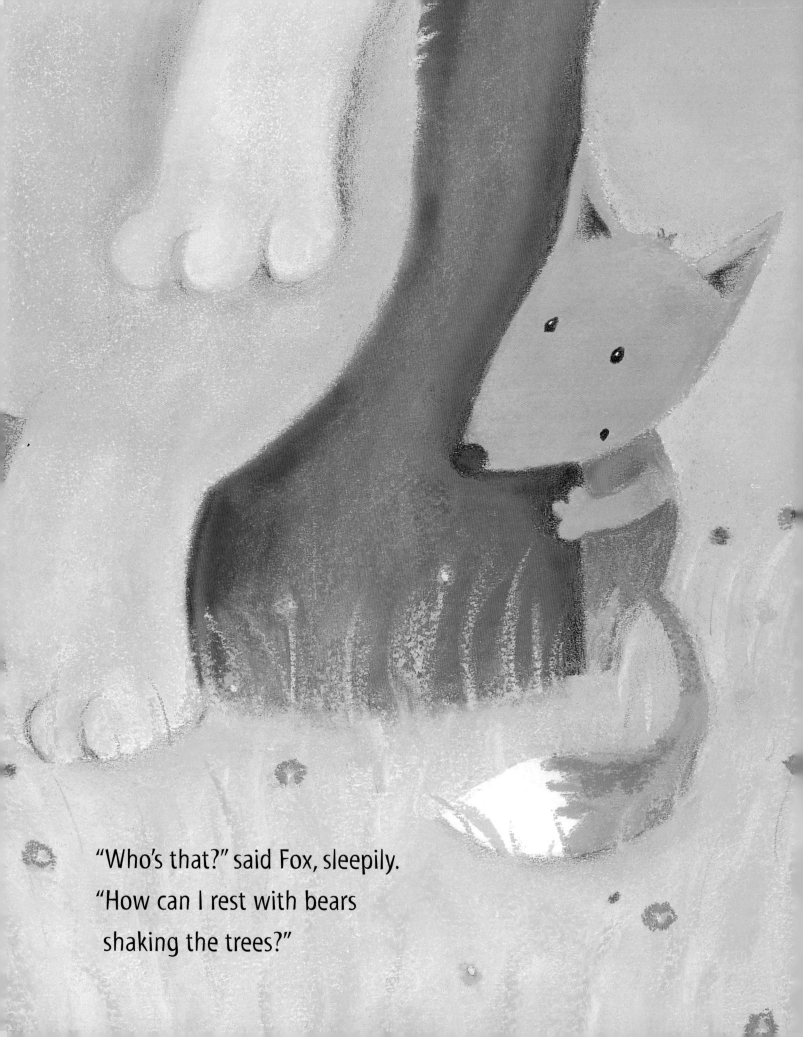

"Who's that?" said Fox, sleepily.
"How can I rest with bears
shaking the trees?"

"Sorry, Fox," said Bear.
"Do you want to scratch
too? It's so nice!"
    But Fox did not
want to scratch,
so Bear clambered
up the tree.

Wheeee!

Wheeee!

Bear swung from branch to branch.
Swinging was one of his favourite
things to do.

Ooops!

Crash! Bear flew into a tree-trunk.
"Yikes!" cried Woodpecker, flying
high into the air. "How can I peck holes
with bears crashing into my tree!"
"Oops! Sorry!" cried Bear, jumping
to the ground.

"Bother! Everyone's too busy to play," Bear thought. "Oh well!" He skipped through the woods, along the riverbank, across the field and back to his favourite hilltop.

Bear lay sunning himself on the hilltop.

Suddenly he heard a loud BUZZZZZZZ!
"Oh no! I'm in trouble again," he thought.

He saw all his friends coming towards him.

"Bear," said Bee, "you're very big…"

"And heavy," said Mole.

"And noisy," said Heron.

"And pesky," said Fox.

"And clumsy," said Woodpecker…

"...But you're really fun.
Let's play!"

"Hoorah!" cried Bear.
Because playing with his friends
really was his favourite thing to do.

Which Little Tiger books do you like best?

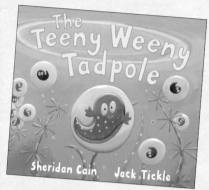

At the End of the
Rainbow

A H Benjamin & John Bendall-Brunello

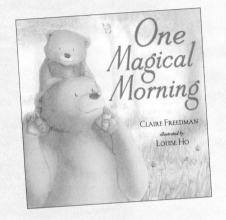

The
Teeny Weeny Tadpole

Sheridan Cain   Jack Tickle

One **Magical Morning**

CLAIRE FREEDMAN
illustrated by LOUISE HO

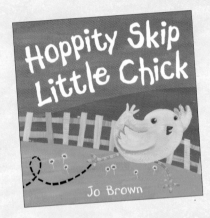

Hoppity Skip Little Chick

Jo Brown

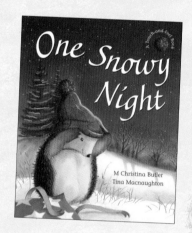

One **Snowy Night**

M Christina Butler
Tina Macnaughton

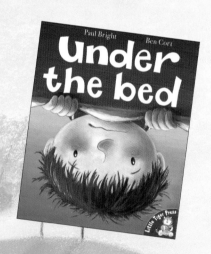

Paul Bright   Ben Cort

under the bed

Little Tiger Press

For information regarding any of the above titles
or for our catalogue, please contact us:
Little Tiger Press, 1 The Coda Centre,
189 Munster Road, London SW6 6AW
Tel: 020 7385 6333 Fax: 020 7385 7333
Email: info@littletiger.co.uk
www.littletigerpress.com